It's me!
love
Tina

Somebody Loves You

by

SCHULZ

CollinsPublishersSanFrancisco

A Division of HarperCollins*Publishers*

How Do I
Love
Thee?

I'd dog paddle the deepest ocean.

Love Makes
You Do
Strange Things

Somebody
Loves You

A Packaged Goods Incorporated Book
First published 1996 by Collins Publishers San Francisco
1160 Battery Street, San Francisco, CA 94111-1213
http://www.harpercollins.com
Conceived and produced by Packaged Goods Incorporated
276 Fifth Avenue, New York, NY 10001
A Quarto Company

Library of Congress Cataloging-in-Publication Data
Schulz, Charles M.
[Peanuts. Selections]
Somebody loves you / by Charles Schulz.
p.   cm.
ISBN 0-00-225158-2
I. Title
PN6728.P4S3278   1996
741.5'973—dc20   96-15819
CIP

Printed in Hong Kong

1 3 5 7 9 10 8 6 4 2